THE WEREWOLF AT DUSK AND OTHER STORIES

THE WEREWOLF AT DUSK

AND OTHER STORIES

DAVID SMALL

Liveright Publishing Corporation

A Division of W. W. Norton & Company
Independent Publishers Since 1923

Printed in China
First Edition

Manufacturing by Toppan Leefung
Production manager: Anna Oler

ISBN 978-1-324-09282-7

Liveright Publishing Corporation
500 Fifth Avenue, New York, N.Y. 10110
www.wwnorton.com

W. W. Norton & Company Ltd.
15 Carlisle Street, London W1D 3BS

1 2 3 4 5 6 7 8 9 0

To Lily, Edison, and Oskar

CONTENTS

INTRODUCTION

THE BEAST WITHIN

THESE THREE STORIES are linked by the dread of things internal: either dread of the turmoil within the characters themselves or, in one case, of a *soul disorder* within the surrounding culture, which only the nameless narrator seems to perceive.

IN LINCOLN MICHEL'S "The Werewolf at Dusk," a miracle of compression and dark humor, the dread is that of a man who has reached a state of crippling old age with something repellant in his nature—in this case, a truly bestial "something"—still intact, untamed.

The idea of the werewolf is an ancient one that leaps from culture to culture and place to place. In "The Werewolf at Dusk," Lincoln gives it a surprising new twist, reminding us that the mental muddles of our youths can—despite maturity and advancing years—still dwell closely, seemingly immutably, within us.

THE SPECTER OF old age also inhabits "A Walk in the Old City," an original story based on a dream that came to me in my mid-seventies, the vestibule of that later stage of life.

I altered the dream to make it work as fiction and, as often happens, the story began to tell me where *it* wanted to go: the protagonist became not me but a psychotherapist in the throes of a midlife crisis.

The doctor, whose professional life rests upon the interpretation of others' dreams, finds himself dreaming, in nesting-doll style, a dream within a dream. Here, the giant spiders—no matter who dreamed them—represent the "beasts within," expressions of the id, our baser instincts, which cannot be rationally explained or easily held back.

THE FINAL STORY is based on Jean Ferry's surrealist tale "Le Tigre Mondain," or "The Tiger in Vogue." I have fleshed out the narrative with near-wordless additions to the beginning and the end, giving readers a better sense of the setting in which the story takes place—Germany in the early 1920s—as well as a broader understanding of the narrator. I've depicted him on his way to what he expects to be a pleasant evening at the music hall, literally bypassing the miseries and violence in the streets of Berlin.

Ferry is long dead. There is no one left to consult about the origins of this story. But it strikes me as the prescient vision of someone who lived through the early days of that period of change and mutability, just before the carnage that swept over Europe. Although Ferry never mentions Adolf Hitler by name, he describes a "little man with the look of a lowly office worker, a little man with pale skin and tired eyes," seated inconspicuously in the loge next to the tiger, whose terrible power he controls using only the power of his will.

Mature readers in 1948 would have no trouble identifying the "little man," for that is how Hitler was perceived when he first appeared, in 1919, in the homes of rich industrialists as a fund-raiser for the newly formed Nazi Party. To liberal observers, he was a clown without then the slightest chance of gaining political power.*

The narrator, as Ferry wrote him, is a common citizen with a touch of clairvoyance. He glimpses something dreadful in the lowbrow entertainment he watches, but he sits among people who seem to be unaware of the danger they are in—or, if they are aware, they eagerly cheer it on. Yet as I have depicted him, the narrator is no hero. He is a classic *Mitläufer*, one who *sees* but walks along, who has no commitment to much of anything beyond the preservation of his own comfort and safety.

The *Mitläufer*, sad to say, is a common beast within. In many ways, Ferry's story is a warning to future generations of an enduring weakness in our nature: to know for certain that things are developing badly, but to let it all slide until salvation is practically beyond reach.

David Small
January 2023

* See Friderich Percival Reck Malleckzewen's *Diary of a Man in Despair*, a book I've read many times, trying to absorb the atmosphere of the times that produced the so-called Age of Monstrosities.

THE WEREWOLF AT DUSK

Story by

Lincoln Michel

I used to wake up in strange places.

Park benches in unfamiliar cities . . .

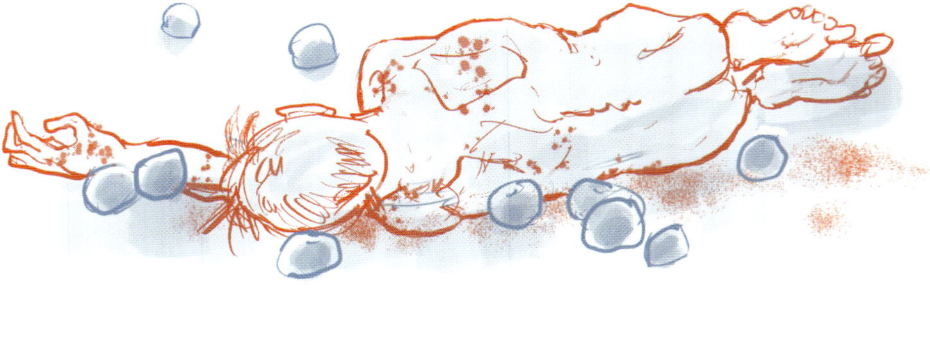

. . . orange groves among the fallen globes.

Suburban backyards . . .

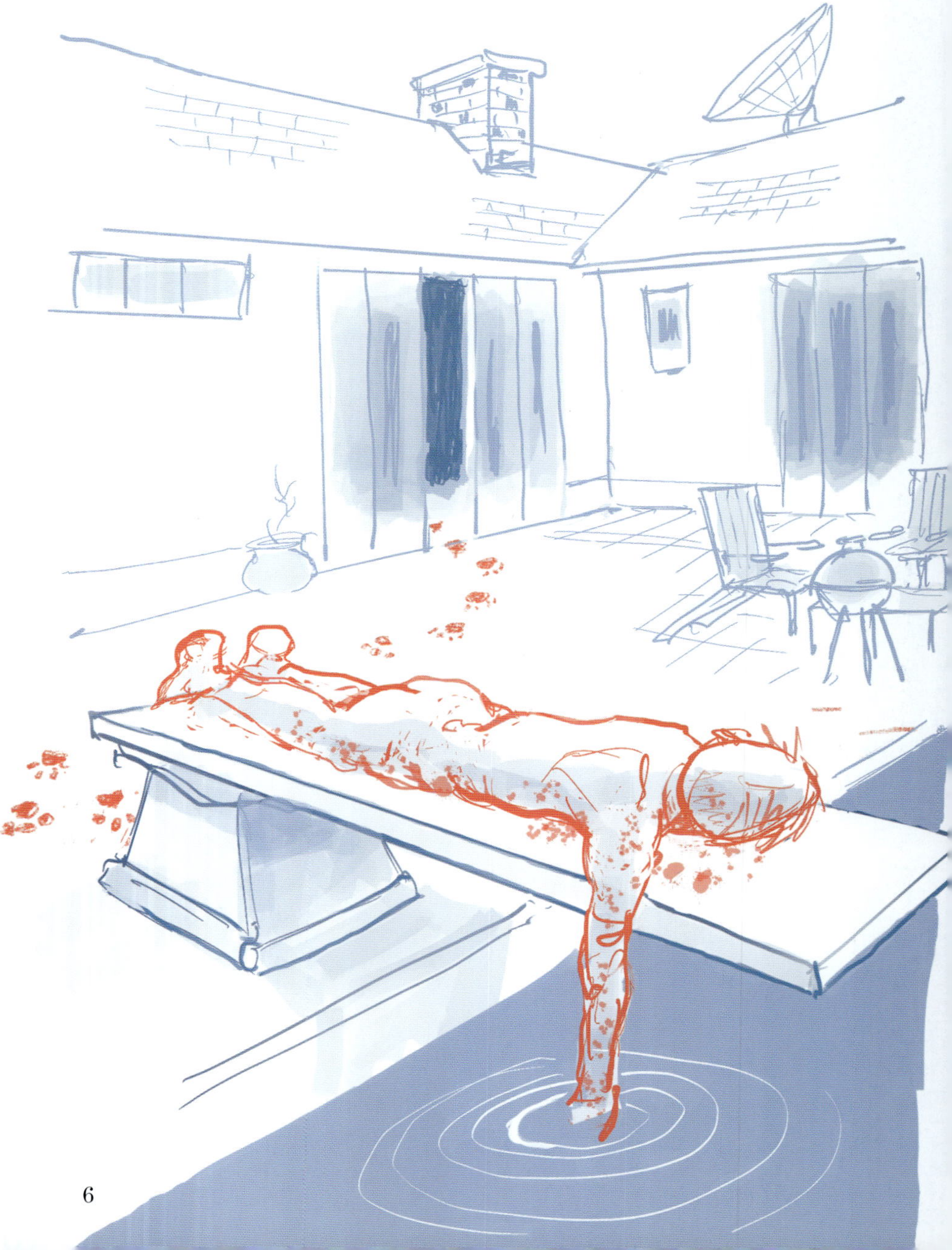

. . . motel parking lots on the edge of dark woods.

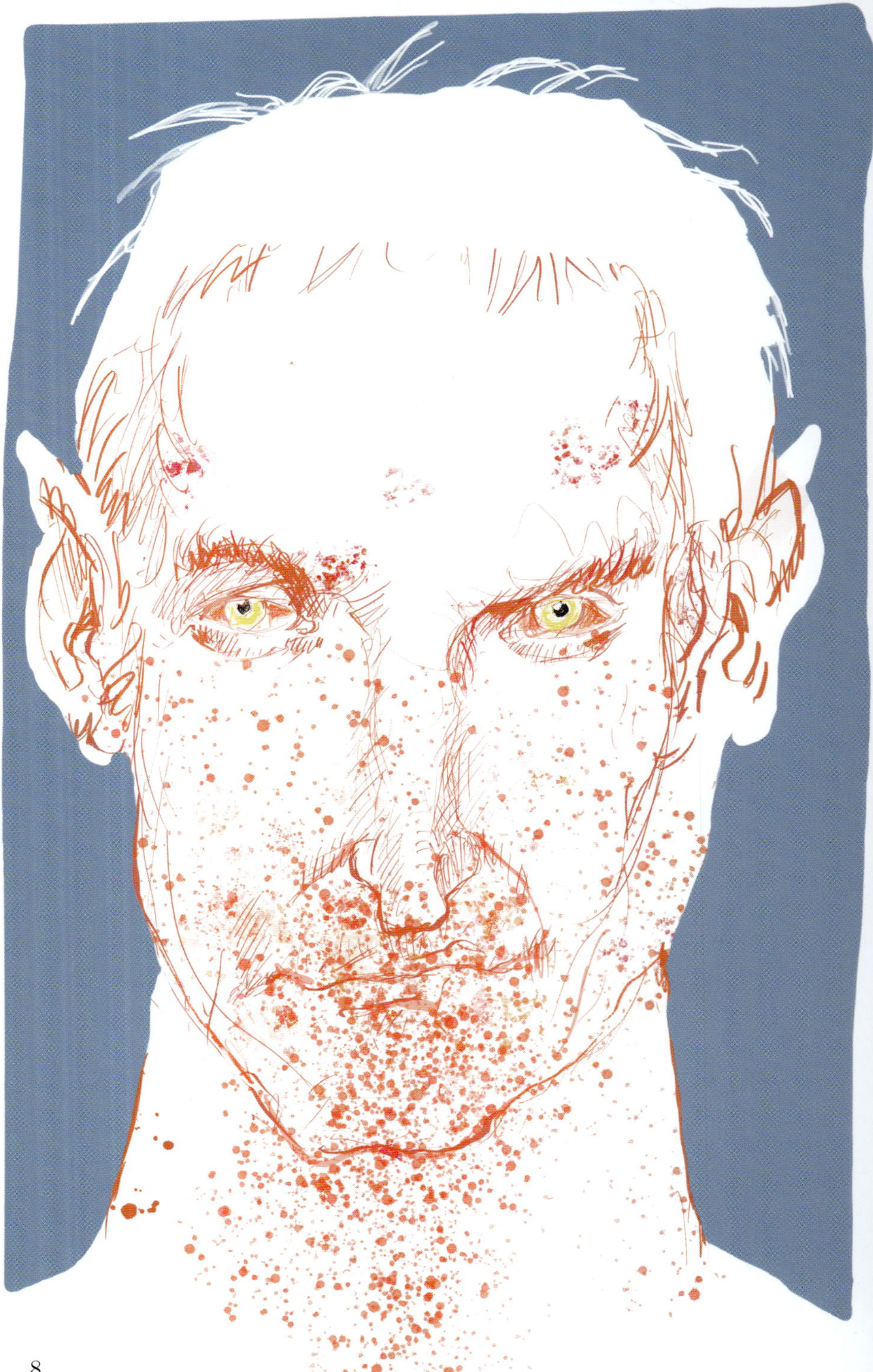

I'd be covered with blood but still alive.

That was a long time ago.

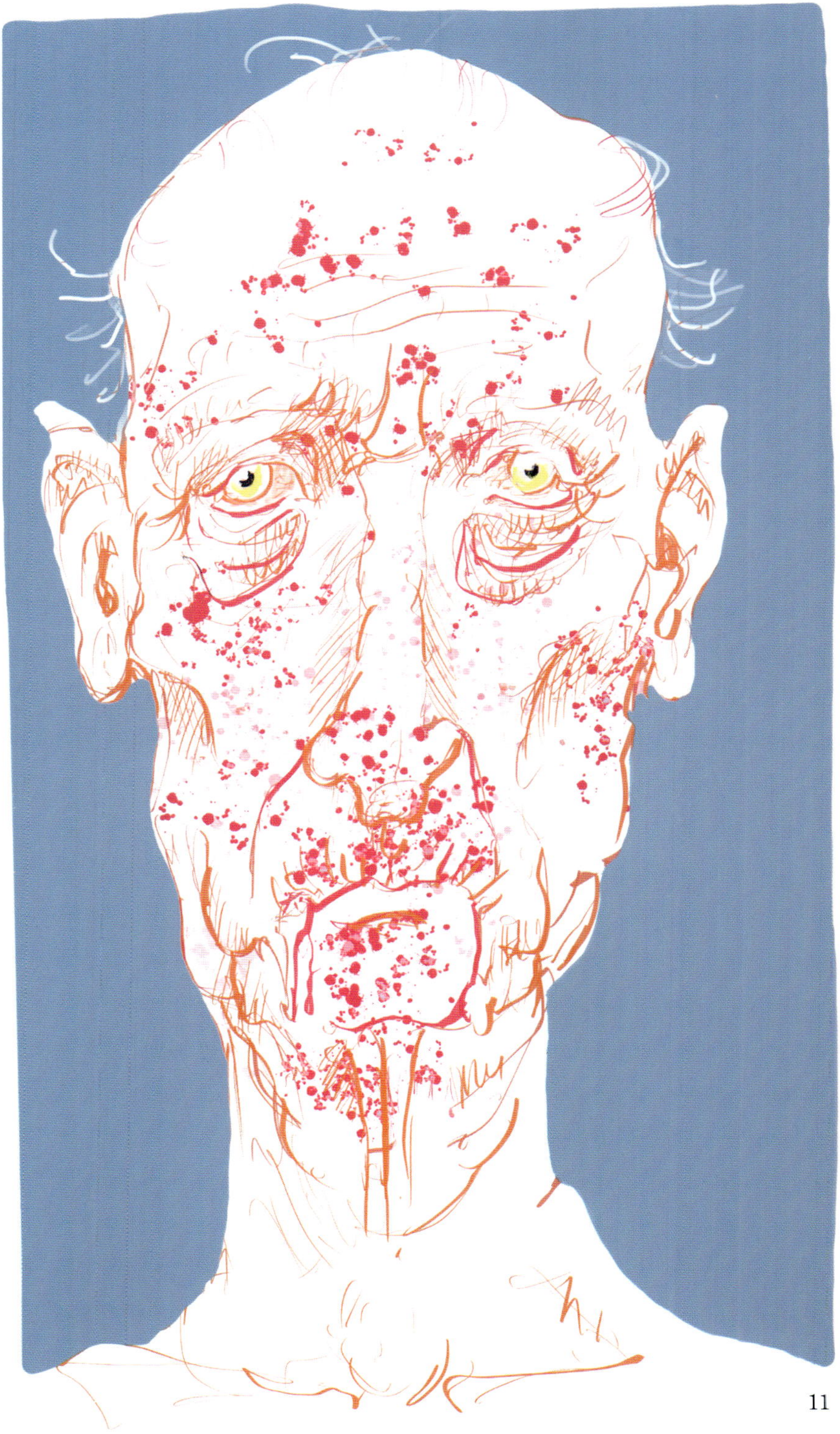

Now, when the moon takes over the sky, I'm lucky if I can overtake an injured squirrel or stumble across a tire-flattened cat.

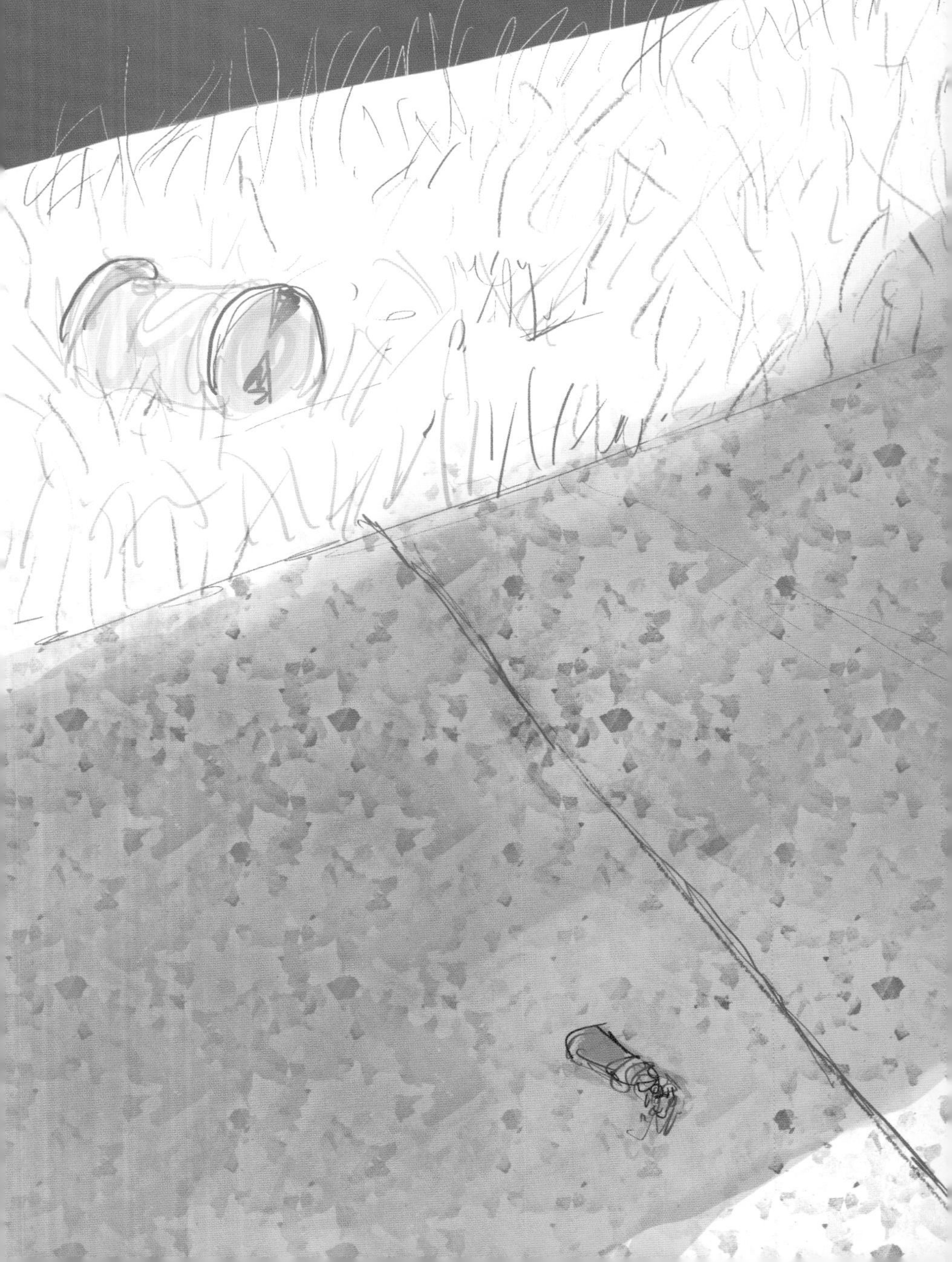

Most mornings I wake up, stomach grumbling, behind dumpsters or crushing flowers in community gardens.

Today it’s a school playground and a policeman shaking his head. “Don’t make me haul you downtown, Gramps. Go home and sober up.”

I manage to hobble home and shower off the blood. Put on a clean pair of jeans and a fresh sweater, then head out again.

A dog walker passes me, a half-dozen mutts barking and straining at their leashes.

My body used to
have that power.

Now it takes me a half hour to get to the store. Sleeping on the playground slide has left me stooped over like a question mark. My knee is inflamed, my hip aches. A small child, barely a snack, has to help me across the street.

I've always feared the moon, ever since I got lost on a family camping trip and heard the howl.

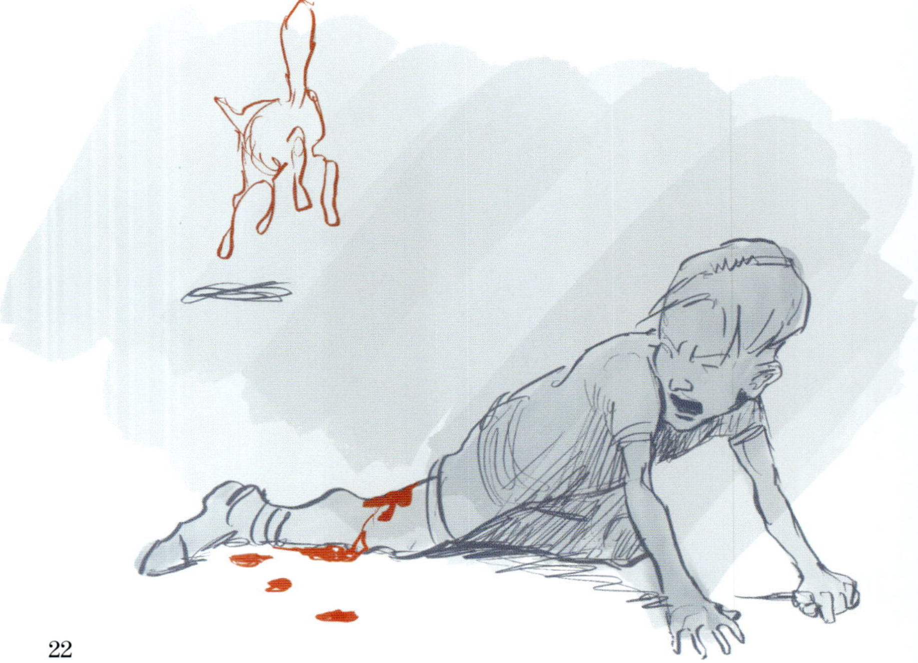

The reason for that fear has changed.
It used to mean I'd hurt other people.

Now it means I hurt myself.

What do I even look like now, when the full moon draws out the wolf inside me?

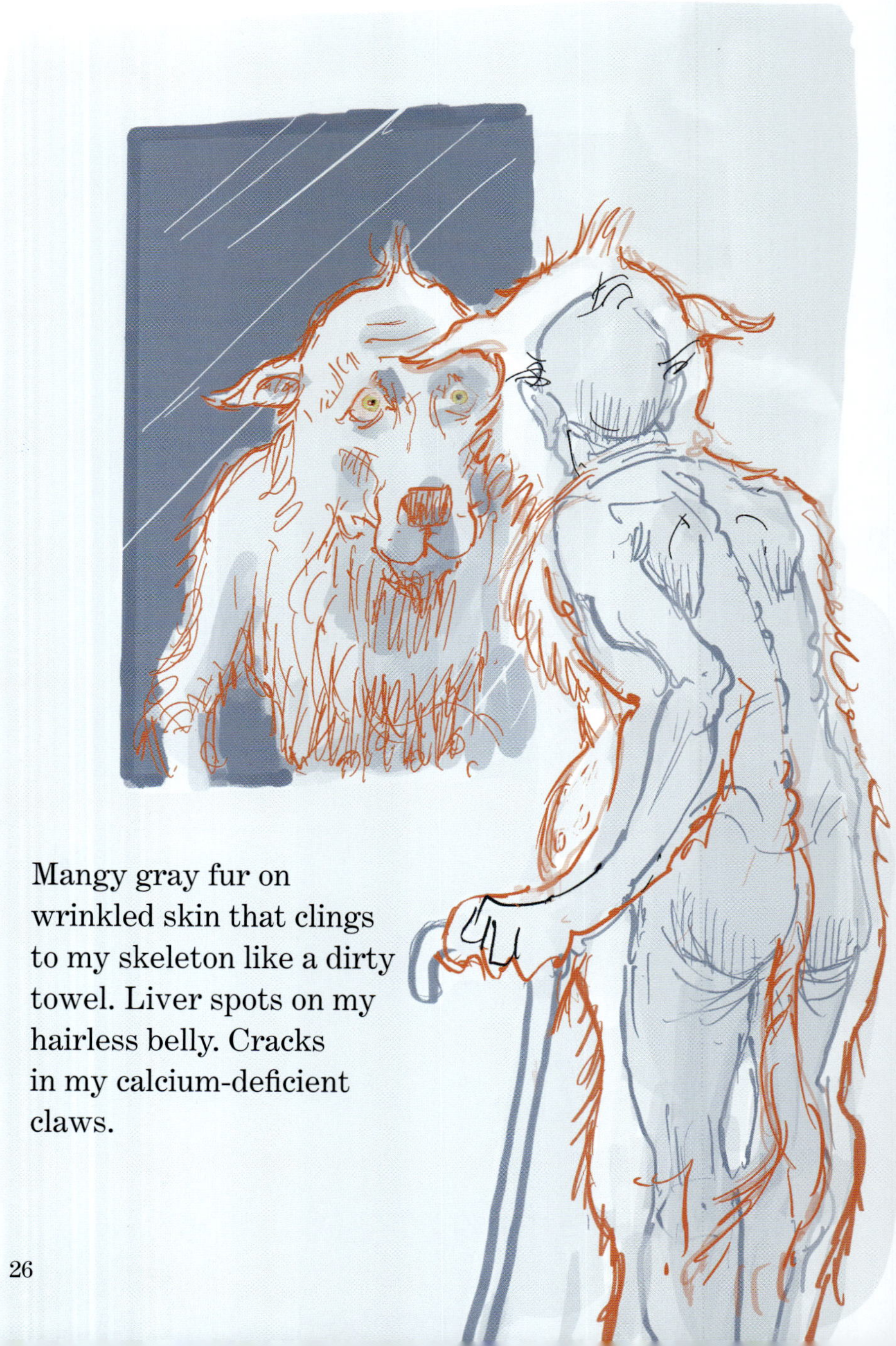

Mangy gray fur on wrinkled skin that clings to my skeleton like a dirty towel. Liver spots on my hairless belly. Cracks in my calcium-deficient claws.

Once I was a monster. Now I'm more a waif than a wolf.

Finally I make it to the local pharmacy.

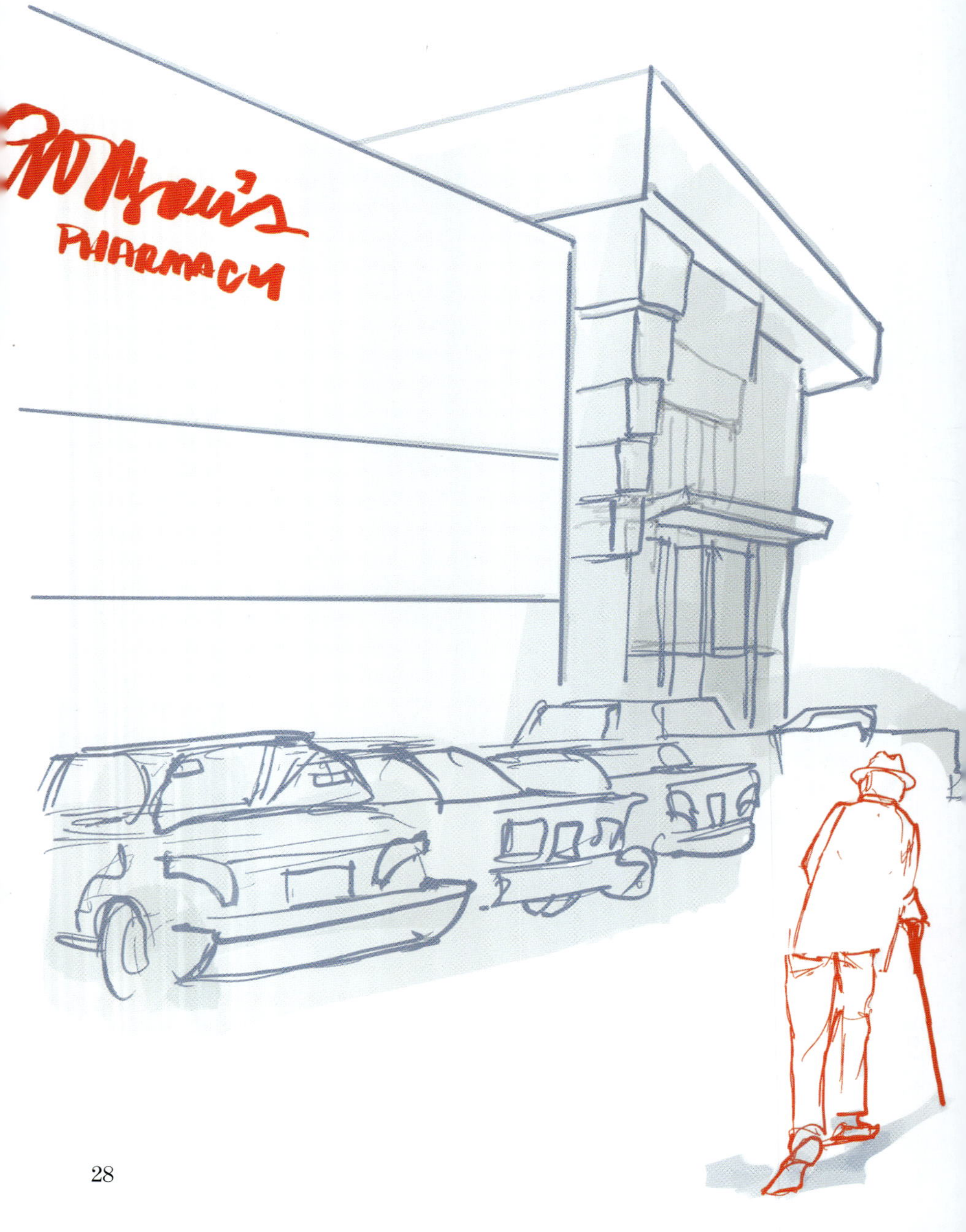

They sell Luna Bars, Moon Pies. My monthly nightmare repackaged as tasty treats.

My trembling hand drops the items on the counter. Advil, Pepto Bismol, Bengay, Band-Aids, ice pack, knee brace. "Looks like grandpa's having a party tonight!" the cashier says. "Don't get too crazy with this stuff. Ha, ha."

He has a flush, round face. Just the right amount of marbling in the muscle.

When I was younger, I would've hidden in the park until he walked home.

I was full of life back then, my whole life ahead of me, like a wide open field to sprint through, the wind in my fur.

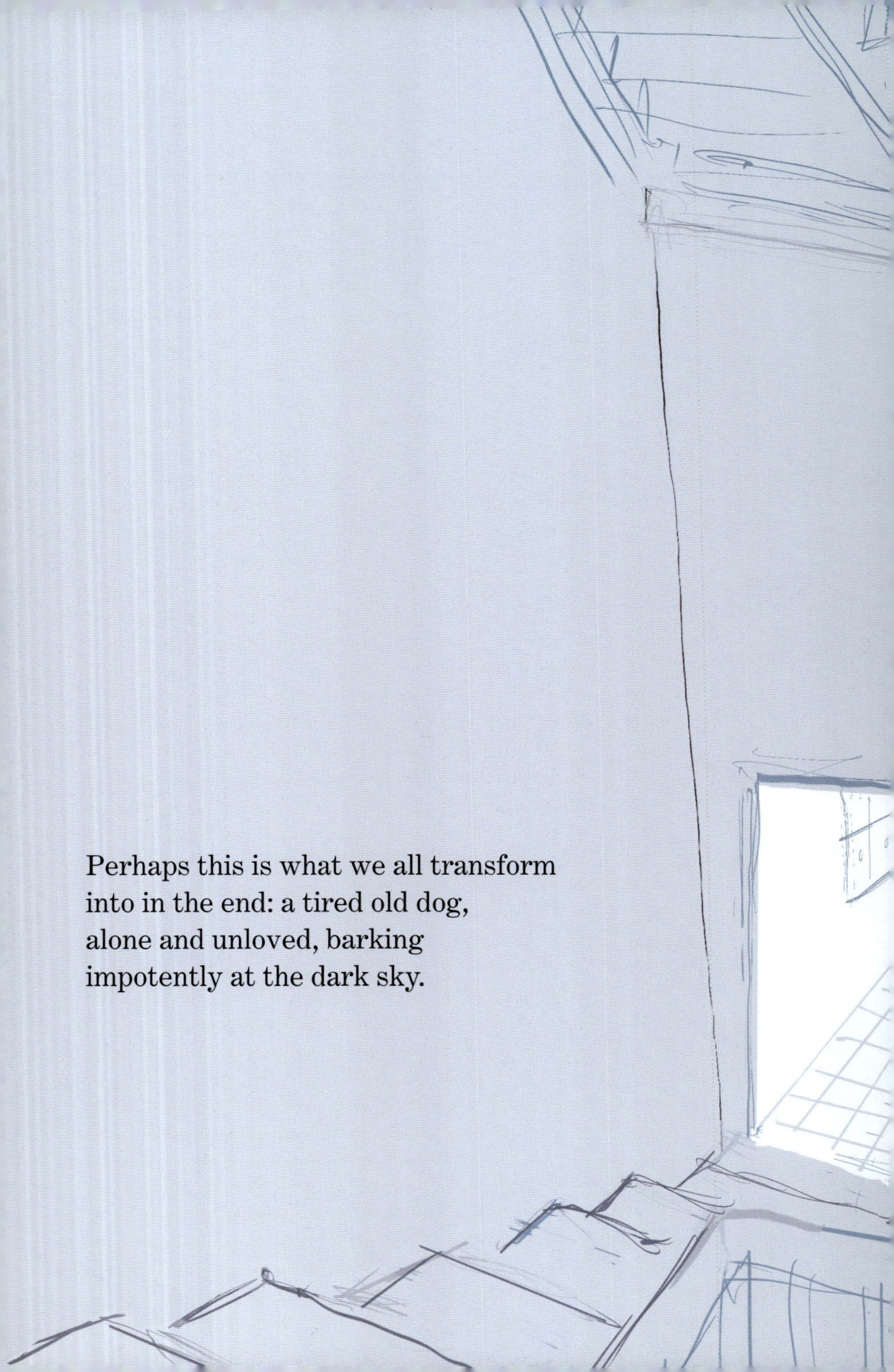

Perhaps this is what we all transform
into in the end: a tired old dog,
alone and unloved, barking
impotently at the dark sky.

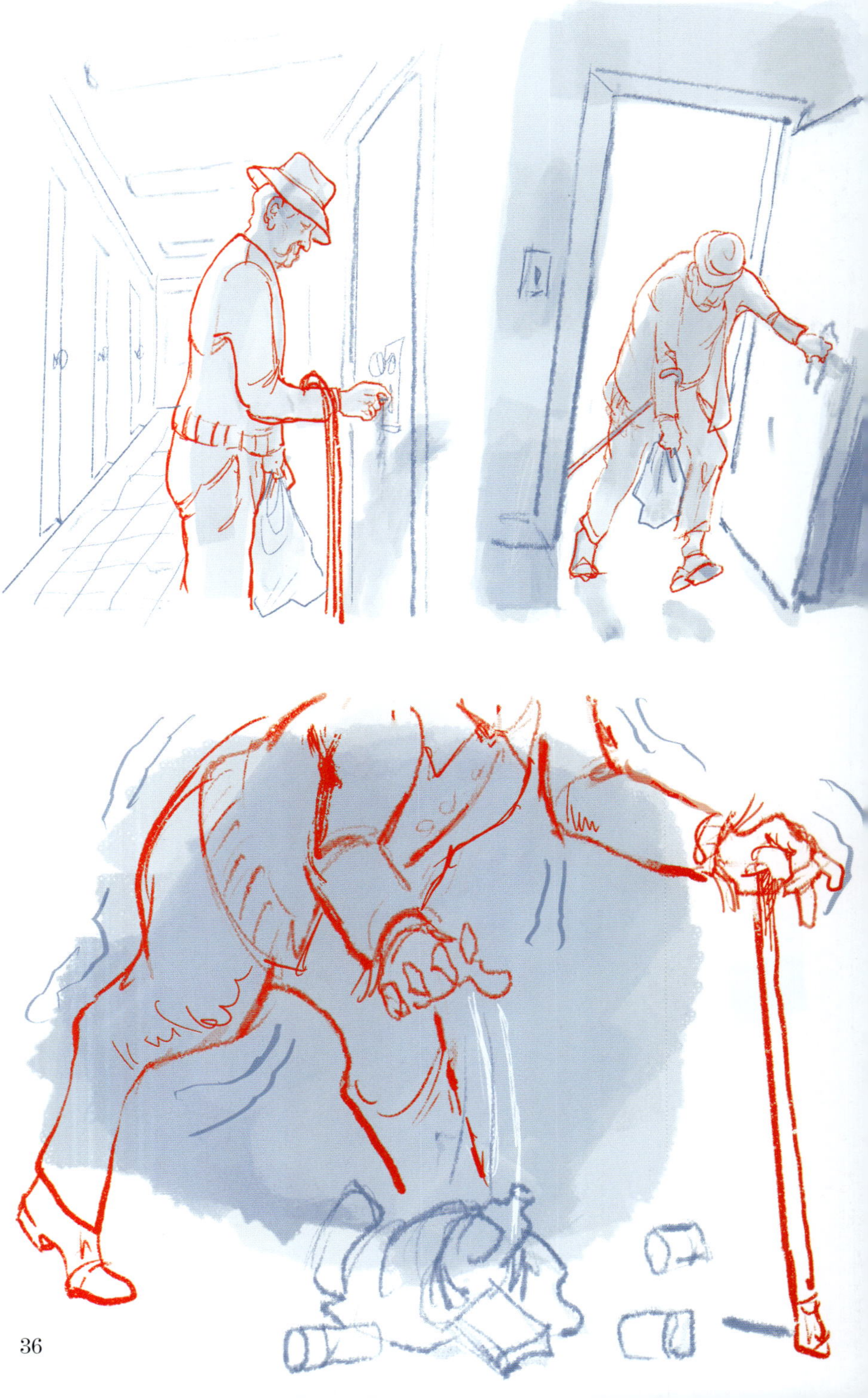

A WALK IN THE OLD CITY

Story by

David Small

It had lately become my habit each afternoon to take long walks, which often found me lost in the Old City.

But getting lost in the Old City was easy. A look at the map will show a tangle of streets like a squashed honeycomb or piece of tripe ground underfoot. These were ancient villages that grew together gradually with no municipal planning. The architecture was the dream of a forgotten time.

I did not speak the local
patois, which led me to a
further sense of being beyond reach,
of having nothing to rely on besides
my own intuition to find my way back.

It was to escape the duplicity of the world that I went on these solitary rambles, prolonging the time I was away and thwarting the cowardly impulse to rush back to stability.

ROWF!
ROWF!
ROWF!

Today I was going in circles.

When this finally occurred to me, I thought of my patients, their inability to see their repetitive behavior. With some of them it covered a span of decades! I was exasperated. Worse, I realized that I had begun questioning my own competence as a psychiatrist and that this doubt was manifesting itself in my behavior. I was dragging myself to work every day, showing up late for appointments and ending them early.

That evening darkness fell early.
The lack of adequate street lighting
made me take several wrong turns
I would not have otherwise made.

At the end of one dark passage I heard the sound of moving water and went toward it.

A sudden rush of vertigo pinned me to the wall and left me there, unable to move.

After some time I became aware of a figure coming toward me.

I'm lost!
Je suis perdu!
¿Me puedes ayudar?

With no indication that he had understood a word, he turned back around and, with a clear gesture, told me to follow.

The bridge, which the old man dared to cross, swayed unsteadily on its rusted bolts and was hung with gigantic spiders, each watching us with its multiple eyes.

I gathered my courage and, imitating the old man, crossed boldly to the other side.

The room we entered, with its spare rough-hewn furnishings, seemed to present the answer to my problems.

As some waggish sage once put it,
"Perhaps, being lost, one should get 'loster'; being very late for an appointment, it might be best to walk slower."

“Here,” I thought, “is a man in total acceptance of his lot, willing to share his meager provisions with a complete stranger. How admirable!”

I could be happy here!

Regardless of the probability that he understood not a word, I went on.
(It was pleasurable to be the talker, not the listener for once.)

As a psychotherapist I quite understand that all of this is a dream. The symbolism is clear:
Being lost in an unfamiliar place? This denotes confusion, perhaps even a feeling of being unloved.
I acknowledge both!
The *old buildings* are my past, in need of revisiting.

The *bridge* represents my need for transition to another state. As I said, I feel lost.
The *black canal* is obviously the River Styx, my fear of death.
BUT . . .

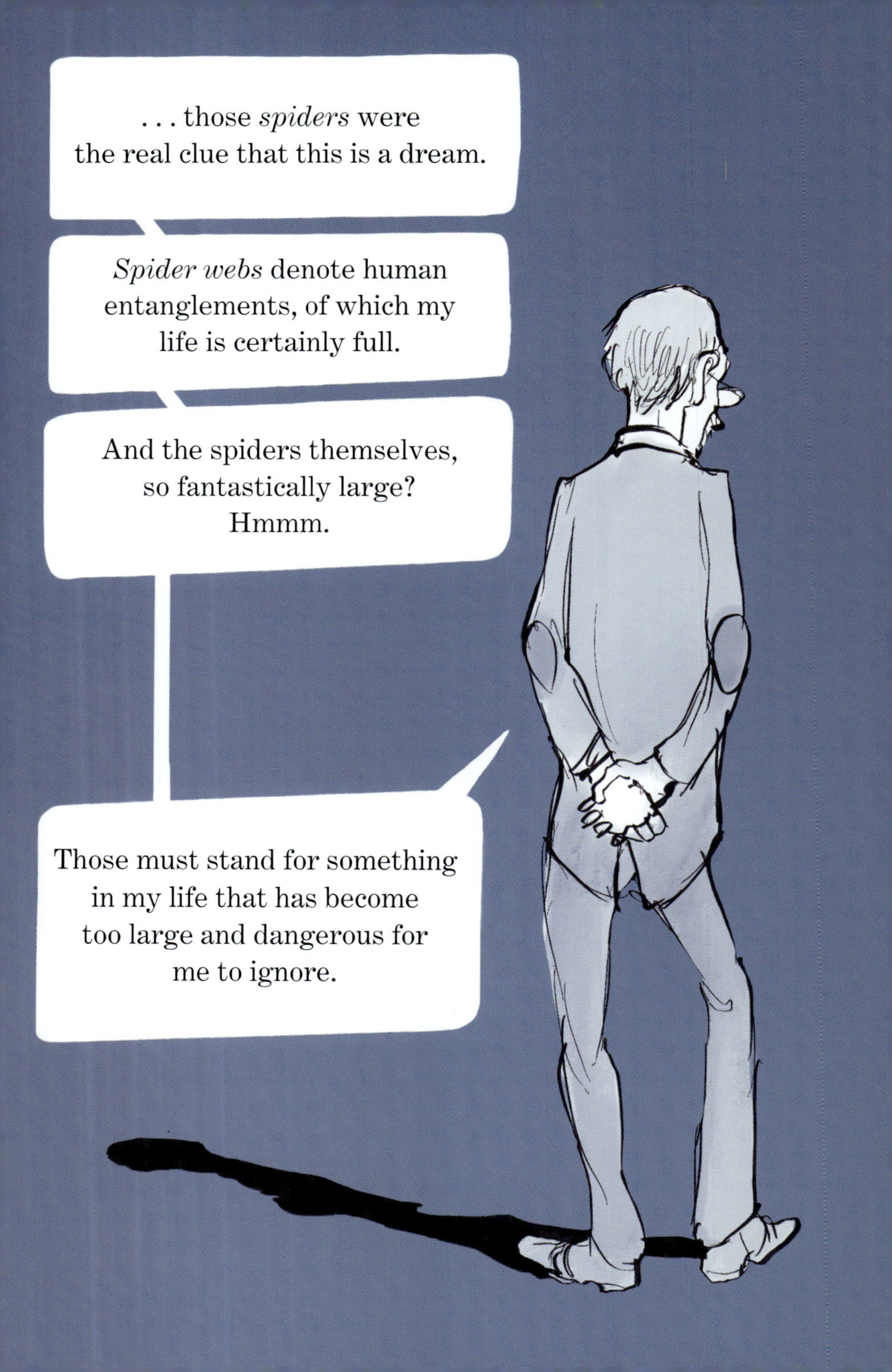
. . . those *spiders* were the real clue that this is a dream.
Spider webs denote human entanglements, of which my life is certainly full.
And the spiders themselves, so fantastically large? Hmmm.
Those must stand for something in my life that has become too large and dangerous for me to ignore.

Could it be the loss of my compassion for my patients?
I'll have to think on that.

I relaxed with that sense of closure that comes from having successfully decoded the metaphors of a difficult dream. I felt at home and at peace . . .

for here I was in the company of a classic dream mentor—old, wise, serene—whose plan was to help me resolve the complexities of life I had devised for myself.

He would help me overcome the inner conflicts that were leading me down so many blind alleys.

But then, glancing up, I saw that the room's rafters were full of huge spiders, just like the ones on the bridge.

As the old man looked at me I saw—for the first time—the pale blue of his irises behind the milk-white veils of thick cataracts. He was blind! His bravery, his stoicism, his acceptance of his miserable condition were all due to blindness!

For the first time he spoke, surprising me with his command of English:
Forgive me, Doctor, but I must tell you that blind people also dream and that our dreams are very similar to the one you just described. We often dream of being lost in strange places, since we always have such difficulty in getting around.
So, who is to say—if this *is* a dream—that it is yours? Why couldn't it be mine?

From the shadows behind him came muffled sounds like heavy sacks of grain hitting the floor.

Spiders are generally solitary creatures. But these are different. They have evolved to adapt to their circumstances.

Against their antisocial nature, here they congregate together to feed and grow fat on the many visitors I bring home.
It’s only fair to tell you—because I despise you people, so smug, so self-satisfied, and so patronizing in your sightedness—these monsters do me a real service.

Let's have a game, shall we? Since it's not in our natures to dream our own deaths, if the dream is yours, you will survive the attack and wake up in the comfort of your own bed to contemplate the symbolism of webs and spiders to your heart's delight.

But . . .
if the dream is mine, you will die and I will wake up, slightly more content than I am now with my miserable lot.

Call my office. You need help!
Not as much as you do, dear Doctor!

Oh! Must you go?
Another time, then?

THE TIGER IN VOGUE

Story by

Jean Ferry

Germany,
early 1920s

VET
VET

BISTRO NIMMERLAND
MENU

MENU

I no longer have the budget for the rich meals
I once enjoyed . . .

. . . but without the occasional visit to the music hall I would feel even more famished.

Even so, a vague menace weighs upon the pleasures I take from the music hall.

If, on examining the bill of fare, I see no mention of a certain act, then I feel free to purchase a ticket and go inside.

I must say, I do enjoy the innocent delights of the dancers, the singers, the jugglers, and magicians.

But when, with no pause, the orchestra strikes up a certain brassy waltz—the ceremonial introduction to that old act "The Tiger in Vogue"—my pleasure abruptly ends. I know what is about to happen.

I should avoid theaters where this number is playing.

Easy to say! For reasons I can never understand, "The Tiger in Vogue" is never announced. It doesn't appear on the program. I never know it's coming.

Or rather, yes, I do.

At the sound of that waltz—knowing full well what it heralds—a sudden crushing weight sits on my chest.

Between my teeth runs the wire of fear, like a bitter low-voltage current.

I should get up and leave, but I don't dare risk it. No one else is moving. No one shares my agony.

Besides, I know the beast is already on its way.

First the theater is plunged into utter darkness.

Then a spotlight comes up to illuminate an empty loge at the edge of the stage.

From there, this pencil of light seeks out the opening of the wings, and while the horns tackle another lively waltz . . .

. . . they enter.

The tiger walks in a fairly human fashion, costumed like an elegant man-about-town. His suit is so perfectly tailored that it's hard to make out the body of the animal beneath.

But then there is the head with its appalling rictus, the crazy eyes rolling in their sockets, the furiously bristling whiskers, and the fangs that glisten under curled lips.

The tamer advances on the arm of her "suitor" toward the empty loge, occasionally making violent efforts to keep him from falling forward.

The whole thing is at once oppressive and slightly comical, but who would think to laugh?

As for me, I watch the tiger, wanting to be somewhere else so badly, I could cry.

Seated, the tiger goes to work, handling props expressly laid out in the loge: a pair of opera glasses through which he pretends to study the audience

. . . and a box of chocolates, which he pretends to share with his companion.

Then, acting the *gallant*, he leans close to the tamer and makes as if to whisper a certain proposition in her ear.

Ooh, la la!

During this farce, my heart beats excruciatingly under my ribs, for I alone see, I alone know that this tasteless spectacle is made possible by a miracle of willpower . . .

. . . that we are all in a state of frightfully unstable equilibrium which a mere trifle could destroy.

What would happen if, in the loge next to the tiger, that little man with the look of a lowly office worker, that little man with pale skin and tired eyes, stopped colluding for one instant?

Because he is the real tamer. The redhead is nothing more than a front.

Everything depends on him. It is he who makes the tiger a marionette, a clockwork toy more tightly bound to him than by cables of steel.

What if the little man, all at once, began to think of something else? What if he died? No one suspects the danger that is possible each second.

It's best not to imagine what the lady would look like if . . . Oh, no, it's best not to imagine.

Better to watch the conclusion of the act, which always ravishes and reassures the public.

There is always some idiot ready to bring a darling little baby up to that demonic box.

While the tiger gazes upon this tasty little morsel with the eyes of a drunk who can't believe his luck . . .

. . . clearly the little man has reached the limits of his strength.

Though no one else is watching him—all eyes being focused on the other loge—I can see that his concentration is nearly drained.

The bogus tamer notices this as well.

Swiftly she returns to baby to its mother and, while the audience erupts in thunderous applause, she and her partner take their bows . . .

. . . exiting quickly, the way they came in.

As soon as they've passed backstage the orchestra breaks into a deafening finale.

Hey, you bastards, Open that cage!

Quick!
He's waking
up!

Having become itself again, released from the bonds of the little man's will, the tiger howls like Hell itself.

It rolls around shredding its handsome clothes, which must be replaced after every show.

Because the hurricane of howls might leave a distasteful impression on the public, the orchestra plays at top volume and the stage manager hurries the burlesque cyclists onto the stage.

YOWL
SLAM!
ROWR
crash!

In her dressing room, the false tamer changes in haste.

The little man, too, seems in a hurry to leave.

As for me, I couldn't get out of there fast enough.

I loathe "The Tiger in Vogue"
and will never understand the
pleasure the public takes from it.

BISTRO NIMMERLAND
MENU

HALT!

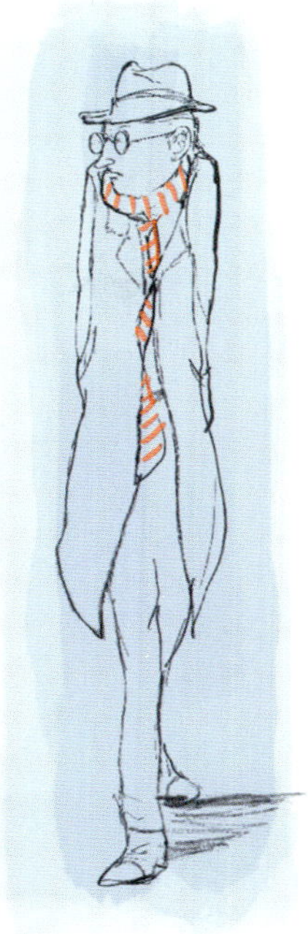

SHUT!

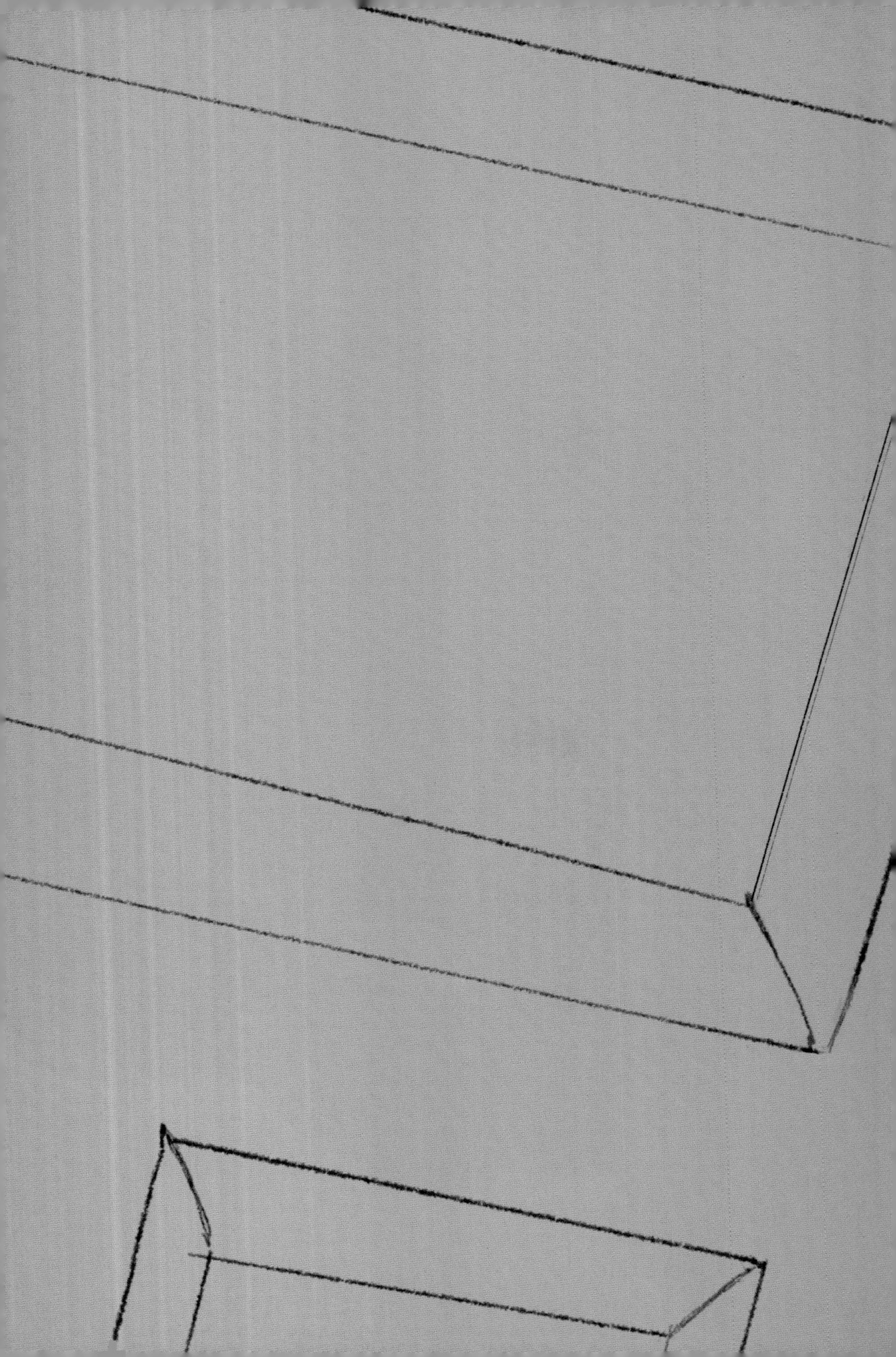

KLIK

Author's Note on "The Tiger in Vogue"

ALTHOUGH HITLER'S Storm Troopers (a.k.a. Brownshirts) were not fully organized until 1931, these armed roughneck insurrectionists were battling leftists and other political opponents and openly assaulting Jews in the streets in the early 1920s, the time when "The Tiger in Vogue" is set. I thought it important, for a swift and wordless identification and to aid the understanding of readers who might be unfamiliar with this history, to put these thugs in full-dress uniform even at this formative stage in their career.

ACKNOWLEDGMENTS

My deepest gratitude goes out to the following people for their suggestions, encouragement, and help on this book:

AT LIVERIGHT
Bob Weil
Haley Bracken
Anna Oler
Sarahmay Wilkinson
Peter Miller
Clio Hamilton

ON THE HOME FRONT
Brenda Bowen
Jon Agee
Patricia Gauch
Brian Evenson
Chafe Hensley
Jennifer Redmann
Kevin Brady
Gerald Cloud
Mark Guin
and, as ever and always,
to my friend/wife
Sarah Stewart

ABOUT THE AUTHOR

DAVID SMALL started his illustration career as an editorial artist for national publications such as *The New Yorker*, the *New York Times*, *Washington Post*, *Esquire*, and *Playboy*. As the author and illustrator of numerous picture books for children, his books have been translated into several languages, made into animated films and musicals, and have won many of the top awards accorded to illustration, including the 2001 Caldecott Medal, two Caldecott Honor Awards, the Society for Illustrators' Gold Medal, and, twice, the Christopher Medal. In 2009, Small's illustration career took a dramatic turn with the publication of his graphic memoir, *Stitches*, which became a *New York Times* bestseller, a National Book Award Finalist, and received the American Library Association's Alex Award. To date, *Stitches* has been translated into ten languages.

Small and his wife, the writer Sarah Stewart, make their home in an 1833 manor house on a bend of the St. Joseph River in Michigan.